Jon Scieszka's TRUCKTOWN on Reading Street

MELVIN SAT

Glenview, Illinois • Boston, Massachusetts • Chandler, Arizona
Shoreview, Minnesota • Upper Saddle River, New Jersey

The gate is down. Stop!

Melvin sat.

Melvin sat, sat, sat.

Trucks have to go!

Go, Melvin, go!